THE FORCE AWAKENS

BY ELIZABETH SCHAEFER   ILLUSTRATED BY DAVID WHITE

Scholastic Children's Books
Euston House,
24 Eversholt Street,
London NW1 1DB, UK

A division of Scholastic Ltd
London ~ New York ~ Toronto ~ Sydney ~ Auckland
Mexico City ~ New Delhi ~ Hong Kong

This book was first published in the US in 2016 by Scholastic Inc.
Published in the UK by Scholastic Ltd, 2016

ISBN 978 1407 16439 7

Book design by Erin McMahon

Printed in Slovakia

1 2 3 4 5 6 7 8 9 10

www.scholastic.co.uk

MIX
From responsible
sources
FSC
www.fsc.org   FSC® C022120

CHANCE TO **WIN**
GO TO LEGO.COM/LIFESTYLE/FEEDBACK
TO FILL OUT A SHORT SURVEY FOR THIS
PRODUCT FOR A CHANCE TO WIN
A COOL LEGO® SET.*

LEGO.com/lifestyle/feedback

THEIR SEARCH TAKES THEM TO THE PLANET OF JAKKU. THERE, AN OLD MAN NAMED LOR SAN TEKKA HAS A MAP TO THE JEDI'S SECRET LOCATION.

NOW WHERE'D I PUT THAT MAP . . .

REY AND FINN ACCIDENTALLY RELEASE DANGEROUS CREATURES FROM HAN'S CARGO HOLD THAT DISTRACT THE GANGS.
BUT I'M TOO PRETTY TO BE EATEN!

WITH THE GANGS OUT OF THE WAY, HAN TAKES EVERYONE TO MEET HIS OLD FRIEND MAZ. SHE OWNS A BIG CASTLE WHERE ALIENS FROM ALL OVER THE GALAXY COME TO HAVE FUN.

MAZ USED TO KNOW LUKE SKYWALKER, AND HAS BEEN KEEPING HIS OLD LIGHTSABER SAFE. REY DOESN'T WANT IT, SO SHE GIVES IT TO FINN.

FINN GETS THE CHANCE TO TRY THE NEW WEAPON SOONER THAN HE WOULD LIKE! THE FIRST ORDER TRACKS THE *MILLENNIUM FALCON* TO MAZ'S CASTLE AND ATTACKS.

FINN, BB-8, HAN AND CHEWIE FLY TO THE RESISTANCE HEADQUARTERS. THERE THEY MEET GENERAL LEIA ORGANA – THE LEADER OF THE RESISTANCE. TOGETHER THEY COME UP WITH A PLAN TO DESTROY THE FIRST ORDER BASE AND RESCUE REY.
I TRIED CALLING. I SWEAR!

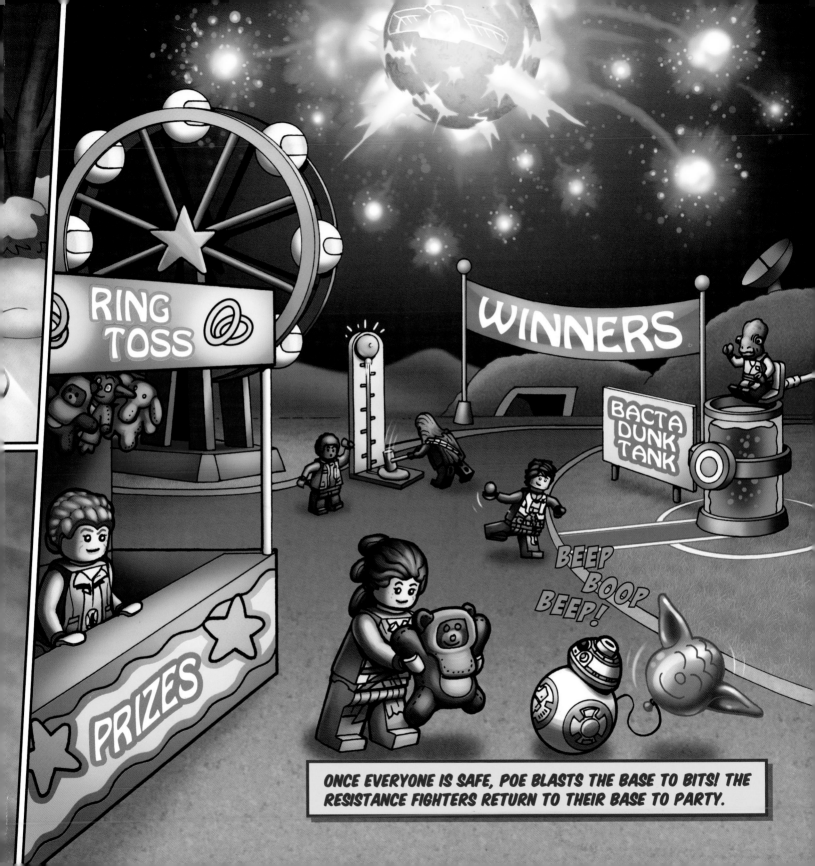

RING TOSS

WINNERS

BACTA DUNK TANK

PRIZES

BEEP BOOP BEEP!

ONCE EVERYONE IS SAFE, POE BLASTS THE BASE TO BITS! THE RESISTANCE FIGHTERS RETURN TO THEIR BASE TO PARTY.